MW00761095

JULIA LEBENTRITT & RICHARD PLOETZ

PICTURES BY CLÉMENT OUBRERIE

HENRY HOLT AND COMPANY • NEW YORK

For Myra Beaton
—J. L. and R. P.

First edition
Published by Henry Holt and Company, Inc.,
115 West 18th Street, New York, New York 10011.
Published simultaneously in Canada by Fitzhenry & Whiteside Ltd.,
195 Allstate Parkway, Markham, Ontario L3R 4T8.

Library of Congress Cataloging-in-Publication Data
Lebentritt, Julia.
The Kooken / by Julia Lebentritt and Richard Ploetz ;
illustrated by Clément Oubrerie.
Summary: Johanna is heartbroken when she goes to practice
her cello for an upcoming concert and finds that Granny's
voracious Doberman pinscher has eaten it.
ISBN 0-8050-1749-6
[1. Dogs—Fiction. 2. Violoncello—Fiction.
3. Grandmothers—Fiction.] I. Ploetz, Richard.
II. Oubrerie, Clément, ill. III. Title.
PZ7.L469Ko 1992
[E]—dc20 91-26826

Printed in the United States of America
on acid-free paper.∞

1 2 3 4 5 6 7 8 9 10

There once was a tall, handsome Doberman pinscher named Kooken who lived with Granny in an old red farmhouse. Granny loved her big dog, but he did have three faults. First, he ate everything. He ate a patchwork quilt, a windowbox of geraniums, and a whole Sunday *Boston Globe*. Second, Kooken never, ever got enough attention. He was always bunting arms and pushing his sleek, heavy head into laps for pets and ear rubs. Especially after he'd done something wrong.

And third, he had trouble with things—crushing them, bumping into them, tipping them over accidentally. Thomas, the cat, had to move from his favorite faded pink hassock to under the stove, where it was safer.

Granny kept her Bible on a high shelf, and nailed the television to the floor. She had little hope that the only Doberman pinscher in North Duxbury, Vermont, would ever settle down and live the peaceful life of a country dog.

One bright June day, a long-awaited guest arrived. Granny's niece, Johanna, rushed up the driveway.

"Good, you brought your cello," Granny said.

"Oh, Gran," Johanna said, in a very excited voice. "The Professor wants me to play in the fall concert—*if* I practice and learn my music!"

Granny smiled. "Well, I hope you'll still have time for swimming, and picking blackberries, and digging me a few fishing worms—and sharing some of my special sour-milk pancakes. Now, run upstairs and put your things away and we'll have supper. And don't leave anything lying about, m'honey girl—" she called after Johanna, "lest you want it chawed to pieces by that big termite."

Kooken pushed open the screen door, came in, and put his nose on the table looking for pancakes.

"You big pest," Granny scolded. "Why don't you go upstairs?" She fixed her eye so sternly on him that he padded quickly out of the kitchen after Johanna.

Kooken stopped outside the bedroom door. Johanna was putting her clothes away in the dresser, humming to herself. She had the softest voice and the friendliest blue eyes. The girl opened her lumpy black suitcase and took out a great wooden thing with a long neck, roundish belly, and strings. She sat in a chair, put an arm around it, and tickled its neck. It chirped! Then, with a stick she'd taken from the black suitcase, Johanna rubbed back and forth across the thing's belly. Kooken's ears cocked up like ragged tulips. It sang—it warbled and howled like a moonstruck dog.

"Johanna, supper!" Granny called from over a pot of steamed dandelion greens and a pan full of red-flannel hash. "Come'n get it!"

Johanna bounded down the stairs, hungry as a girl fresh to the country can be.

Kooken watched the shiny creature a long while, but it didn't move from where Johanna had leaned it in the corner. Probably fast asleep from such special petting, he thought. He approached timidly, stuck out his nose, and gave a sniff.

The creature let out such a dark, windy groan that the Doberman's hair stood up as tall as it could—an eighth of an inch.

Wiping her plate with a slice of homemade bread, Johanna told Granny all about the concert. It was held every year in Carnegie Hall, and the best music students were chosen to perform.

"It sounds like a big deal, all right," Granny agreed, looking at Johanna. "And you deserve it. You've been playing that cello since you were knee-high to it."

A sound like thunder made the silverware jingle in the drawer. Johanna looked up, startled.

"Probably one of those lumber trucks coming down the hill road," Granny said.

They finished supper and did the dishes. Then Johanna went upstairs to practice while Granny put the kettle on.

The little bedroom looked like it had been turned upside down! The night table lay on its side. The rug had been wadded into a clump and the bed shifted from one corner to the other. The fresh daisies were in a puddle of water. And there was a ball of knotted strings and splinters in the middle of the floor. . . .

"My CELLO!" Johanna sobbed. "What will I do? I can't afford another cello! The concert in September . . . oh, Granny!"

Granny called Kooken out from under the bed. "You—WORM!" she uttered. He wiggled miserably and crept up beside Johanna, craned his neck, and made his eyes big and sorrowful like saucers full of hot chocolate. He laid his head lightly in her lap. Without thinking, the girl rubbed his ears.

"*Arrrrrrr* . . ." Kooken couldn't help growling with pleasure.

Granny eyed him sternly. "We ought to sell you and buy Johanna another cello—except *you* wouldn't bring fifty cents!" And she stormed back down to the kitchen to get the tea.

Kooken flicked his ears hopefully twice and bumped Johanna's arm with his wet nose.

"Oh, it's all right," she said gloomily, putting her arm around the big dog's neck. "You didn't mean to wreck my cello. You're just—just—Kooken." She scratched his chest a little.

Kooken lifted his head and gave a long, drawn-out *"Oooo-ooo-ooo-ooo."*

Johanna stared at him.

"Darned if that didn't sound like a cello." Granny set the teapot on the dresser. "Without my specs, he sort of looks like your cello. Here—" Granny handed Johanna her cello bow. "Give him a try."

"Oh, Gran—" But Johanna's arm stayed around Kooken's long, graceful neck. She rubbed across his chest with the bow.

"DOHHHHHHHHHHHHH . . ." The windowpanes vibrated.

Kooken's lush black body shone like polished wood. Johanna bowed expertly across his belly while fingering his throat with her other hand. *"Do—re—mi—fahhh—"* Kooken stretched his neck: *"So—la—ti—DOHHHHHH . . ."*

"He has a fabulous tone," Johanna whispered. "Gran, he's a Stradivarius cello!"

Johanna spent the whole happy summer playing the Kooken. In the past she'd been a little lazy in her cello study, but the Kooken was always putting his head in her lap and bunting, reminding her it was time to practice. He learned to throw back his head and sing in four keys, major and minor. When Johanna fingered his left ear, he could hit high C. When she pulled out his right ear and bowed across it, he sang arpeggios in harmonics. When she bowed him with short, quick strokes below the belly button, he rolled his eyes and droned tremolo. He loved being played, and his favorite piece was Debussy's *Afternoon of a Faun*. He would fall into a reverie after two measures and dream of dainty Doberman princesses and very large bones . . .

Johanna could hardly believe the summer was over and it was time to go back to New York City. Then she remembered—they didn't allow dogs on the trains.

"Well, he didn't eat your cello case," Granny said with a grin. Johanna fetched the case. "Cut four holes in the bottom," Granny ordered. They tried the case on the Kooken.

"Now, you old foghorn," Granny instructed her pet, "lie low on the train, and sing like a thrush for the Professor. And," she added sternly, thinking of the cellos the Professor might own, "never, *ever* eat another cello—they're your brothers."

In New York City no one even stopped to stare. They supposed, if they gave it any

thought, that Johanna was just another world-famous cellist with a cello that walked.

At the music school, Johanna snapped open the case and the Kooken stepped out.

The Professor blinked his eyes behind little square spectacles.

"This is the Kooken," Johanna began. The Kooken scratched his ear, thumping the floor so it shook.

"Kuchen, hmm? Back in Austria, when I said 'kuchen,' I meant pancake." The Professor peeked inside the case. "Nice dog . . . but, Miss Johanna, *no cello?*"

"Oh, Professor—I've practiced all summer with the Kooken—"

"Now, now, my girl, I have no time for nonsense—show me what you can do with this!" The Professor pulled a cello from the corner. It was *the* very old and valuable cello, which only his outstanding students were permitted to play.

"Oh, Professor," Johanna stammered, holding the famous cello.

"And you, Mr. Pancake," the Professor said, giving the Kooken a little push, "sit out of the way, please."

This cello felt light as a bird in Johanna's arms. What an honor! She picked up her bow and played carefully at first—and then with great spirit.

A smile spread over the Professor's face. His right foot began to tap—and suddenly he was waltzing around the studio, coattails flying.

Kooken watched and listened. Black thoughts were storming in his head; he wanted to eat this valuable cello right here. He padded over to the open window and stared down over a box of geraniums at the gray city.

When Johanna finished playing, the Professor sat for a few moments panting on the edge of the piano bench. At last he spoke: "You will play the cello in the concert."

"Oh, Professor!" Johanna stood.

"Now, now," said the Professor. "But please, get that dog to stop eating my geraniums."

Carnegie Hall was packed. Johanna was third on the program. She tried to concentrate on her music, but all she could think of was Kooken. It had been a week of disasters since that day at the Professor's. Kooken had flattened one of her mother's antique Chippendale chairs, eaten her father's Black Forest cuckoo clock, and caused the downstairs neighbors to report an earthquake to the weather bureau. Johanna hadn't dared leave Kooken alone in her parents'

apartment this evening of the concert. So she snuck him in as her second cello and left him in the dressing room. "Be good, *please*," she had whispered, shutting the door. She *had* to concentrate. Granny would have to take him home after the concert. There was the sound of applause—it was *her* turn!

Johanna took her place on stage. The audience stretched out in a vast sea of faces. She started to draw her bow, but her hand was shaking.

There was a terrible silence.

"Play!"
the Professor
whispered fiercely
from the wings.
She could not.
It was as if her
arms were made
of lead.
"Play! Play!" The
Professor shook his fists.
But she couldn't—
it was as if steel gloves
held her hands.
"Stage fright!" the
Professor whimpered
with his head in his hands.

Suddenly a big dog galloped onto the stage, saw the girl, skidded to a stop, and scrambled straight for her.

Cries of terror came from the audience.

"Kooken!" Johanna laid the cello down. Kooken bumped Johanna's arm with his wet nose and flicked his ears. She put her arm around the big dog's neck and scratched his chest.

Kooken lifted his head and gave a long, drawn-out *"Oooo-ooo-ooo-ooo."*

The audience stared. There were whispers: "Darned if that didn't sound like a cello . . ." "Sort of looks like a cello . . ."

"Play!" the Professor shouted, meaning the cello, but Johanna's arm was around the big dog's neck. She looked happily at Kooken. She knew her music and so did he. With a flourish she lifted her bow. The Kooken raised his great, sleek head and they began to play.

TAXI

They played everything they knew from the long summer's practice—Bach, Schubert, Mozart, Ives . . . and then a few spontaneous pieces about birds and deer, black-and-white cows in green pastures, sun-ripe blackberries, and the brook that tumbled down past Granny's. . . .

The crowd roared. There was a standing ovation. Three encores. People were throwing flowers and hats and programs, whistling and bravoing, when all at once—fat golden pancakes began floating down onto the stage, onto the cheering people.

"*YOOHOO!*" Johanna cried, waving her bow.

"*HOOOOOOOO!*" the Kooken bayed, not sounding like a cello at all.